This book belongs to

....

For Hunter and Hero

MY BROTHER IS A VAMPIRE

First published in Great Britain in 2021 by Kirstin McNeil in collaboration with

Sequoia Publishing UK   Snap Shot Productions ltd

www.sequoiapublishing.co.uk   www.snapshotproductionsltd.com

Text & illustrations copyright © Kirstin McNeil 2021

A catalogue record of this book is available from the British Library.

ISBN: 978 1 9168803 0 6
Printed in the UK

My Brother is a Vampire

Kirstin McNeil   Steven Bristow

My brother is a vampire,
he doesn't like the sun.
He's always waking up at night
annoying everyone.

But no one ever listens,
and no one else agrees.
My brother is a VAMPIRE.
Help me please!

My brother is a vampire,
his fangs are super spiky.
They cut through all the toughest toys,
I hope he doesn't bite me!

But I'm the only one that knows it,
the only one that sees
that my brother is a VAMPIRE.
Help me please!

My brother is a vampire,
he has my parents in a trance.
They walk around like zombies
as he makes them sing and dance.

But they say I'm being silly!
They think I'm trying to tease.
My brother is a VAMPIRE.
Help me please!

My brother is a vampire,
his best friend is a ghoul.
He messes up my bedroom
whenever I'm at school.

But my teachers don't believe me.
Not even Mr Rees.
My brother is a VAMPIRE.
Help me please!

My brother is a vampire,
he only eats red food.
He throws it at my Mum and Dad,
it's incredibly rude.

My brother is a vampire,
he sleeps the wrong way round.

I'm sure I saw him fly one night,
he loves being upside down.

Oh, will someone ever listen?
I'm begging on my knees!
My brother is a VAMPIRE.
Help me please!

My brother is a vampire,
he doesn't cry, he shrieks!
It's loud and wierd and spooky
and it's giving me the creeps.

But no one else can understand it.
Nobody believes!
My brother is a VAMPIRE.
Help me please!

My brother is a vampire,
but I don't want him fixed...

...Because whilst they're watching him all day,
I'm up to naughty tricks!

Can You Spot?

Brothers Hunter and Hero have hidden these items in this book. Can you spot them?

Author Kirstin loves to crochet toys from wool. Can you spot the bat?

In memory of Peter Baldwin, and to raise awareness of the #knowtype1 diabetes campaign.

Where's Hero's graffiti tag? Can you spot any other graffiti?

Digby is the headmaster's dog at Hunter's school.

This was the picture that inspired the whole book!